Dear Parent:

Congratulations! Your child is taking the first steps on an exciting journey. The destination? Independent reading!

STEP INTO READING® will help your child get there. The program offers five steps to reading success. Each step includes fun stories and colorful art. There are also Step into Reading Sticker Books, Step into Reading Math Readers, Step into Reading Phonics Readers, Step Into Reading Write-In Readers, and Step Into Reading Phonics Boxed Sets—a complete literacy program with something to interest every child.

Learning to Read, Step by Step!

Ready to Read   Preschool–Kindergarten
• big type and easy words • rhyme and rhythm • picture clues
For children who know the alphabet and are eager to begin reading.

Reading with Help   Preschool–Grade 1
• basic vocabulary • short sentences • simple stories
For children who recognize familiar words and sound out new words with help.

Reading on Your Own   Grades 1–3
• engaging characters • easy-to-follow plots • popular topics
For children who are ready to read on their own.

Reading Paragraphs   Grades 2–3
• challenging vocabulary • short paragraphs • exciting stories
For newly independent readers who read simple sentences with confidence.

Ready for Chapters   Grades 2–4
• chapters • longer paragraphs • full-color art
For children who want to take the plunge into chapter books but still like colorful pictures.

STEP INTO READING® is designed to give every child a successful reading experience. The grade levels are only guides. Children can progress through the steps at their own speed, developing confidence in their reading, no matter what their grade.

Remember, a lifetime love of reading starts with a single step!

For Erik—You put the "Ka-chow!" in my life!
—S.A.

Materials and characters from the movie *Cars 2*. Copyright © 2011 Disney/Pixar. Disney/Pixar elements © Disney/Pixar, not including underlying vehicles owned by third parties; and, if applicable: Hudson Hornet, Jeep® and the Jeep® grille design are registered trademarks of Chrysler LLC; Mercury and Model T are trademarks of Ford Motor Company; Porsche is a trademark of Porsche; Sarge's rank insignia design used with the approval of the U.S. Army; Volkswagen trademarks, design patents and copyrights are used with the approval of the owner, Volkswagen AG; FIAT is a trademark of FIAT S.p.A.; Chevrolet Impala is a trademark of General Motors. Background inspired by the Cadillac Ranch by Ant Farm (Lord, Michels and Marquez) © 1974. All rights reserved. Published in the United States by Random House Children's Books, a division of Random House, Inc., 1745 Broadway, New York, NY 10019, and in Canada by Random House of Canada Limited, Toronto, in conjunction with Disney Enterprises, Inc.

Step into Reading, Random House, and the Random House colophon are registered trademarks of Random House, Inc.

Visit us on the Web!
StepIntoReading.com
www.randomhouse.com/kids

Educators and librarians, for a variety of teaching tools, visit us at
www.randomhouse.com/teachers

ISBN: 978-0-7364-2808-8 (trade) — ISBN: 978-0-7364-8101-4 (lib. bdg.)

Printed in the United States of America 10 9 8 7 6 5 4 3 2 1

DISNEP · PIXAR

RACE
AROUND
THE
WORLD

By Susan Amerikaner

Illustrated by the Disney Storybook Artists

Random House 🏠 New York

Lightning is a race car.

He is fast!

Lightning is a big star.

A car from Italy
is fast, too.

Who is faster?

The cars will race!

The first race is
in Japan.

The car from Italy
is the winner.

Lightning is not happy.

The second race is
in Italy.

Both cars want

to win!

One car spins
on the track!

Lightning wins!

The third race is
in Radiator Springs.
It is the last race.

The cars line up.

The fans are ready.

The cars race!

The fans cheer.

Go, Lightning, go!

Who will win?